The Princess without a CROWN

Printed in the United Kingdom
First Printing, 2020

ISBN: Print (Soft Cover): 978-1-912677-90-0

Published by Purple Parrot Publishing

www.purpleparrotpublishing.co.uk

For all the Princesses out there who know their own mind and are one of a kind.

Especially Bella the Brave, Marvellous Marleigh and, of course, Princess Lottie.

Remember: don't just think outside the box, think like there is no box!

A princess should always wear a CROWN, even for a trip to town.

"No way," said Princess Lottie.

A princess must always wear a dress, diamonds, rubies, and look her best.

"NAH," said Princess Lottie.

A princess should always smell divine,
lotions, potions, quite sublime.

"Not quite," said Princess Lottie.

Princesses are oh so quiet and mild,
never, ever are they loud and wild.

"**Really?**" said Princess Lottie.

A princess will have lots of friends,
a busy life with **girls'** weekends.

"I like me," said Princess Lottie.

Princesses like a tasty treat,
delicious food they like to eat.

"Exactly!" said Princess Lottie.

This princess likes the colour pink.

You'll **never** find her at the sink.

"I like being *busy*," said Princess Lottie.

To do
paint poster
visit Grandma
shopping
gardening
help at library
deliver cakes

All princesses like a ball,

ballgowns, slippers, coaches all.

"I love this b𝐚ll," said Princess Lottie.

Princesses should be seen, not heard,
and never have the final word.

"HEAR MY **VOICE**," said Princess Lottie.

A princess will always be polite,
especially to a *handsome* knight.

"Hmmmm," said Princess Lottie.

A princess should always know her mind,
be true to herself - she's one of a kind!

"Yes!" said Princess Lottie.

Lightning Source UK Ltd.
Milton Keynes UK
UKHW050252181122
412370UK00001B/3